Kevin's Christmas

Liesbet Slegers

Clavis

NEW YORK

Hi, I am Kevin.

We have a tree at my house.

But it is not outside;

it is inside the house.

It is not a tree with leaves;

it has many needles and it smells sweet and spicy.

Why would my parents have a tree inside?

"Well, Kevin, what do you think of our
Christmas tree?" Mommy asks.
"We are going to decorate it. Will you help us?"
She shows me a big box of decorations—shiny
balls, little lights, and a golden star
for the top of the tree!
Oh, it is sparkling and beautiful—a real
Christmas tree!

I help Daddy put a nativity scene under the tree. All the little figures have their own special place: The little baby Jesus, his mother Mary, his father Joseph, the cow, and the donkey. Daddy tells me Jesus was born on Christmas and we celebrate his birthday during this holiday.
I lay the baby Jesus in the warm straw.

Mommy and I go outside to the mailbox. It is filled with greeting cards from our family and friends, all wishing us a Merry Christmas and a happy New Year. I helped send out greeting cards to everyone, too!

When we're back inside, I decide to make a present for my cousin, Sally.

I make her a necklace out of string and beautiful beads the colors of the rainbow.

I put it in a box and tie a ribbon around it.

Then I put it under the Christmas tree.

I hope she likes it!

Mommy and I go grocery shopping. I'm going to help prepare a great big Christmas feast later! I have my own grocery cart to wheel around the aisles and we buy delicious things: Sparkling cider, turkey, apples, chocolate ice cream ... Yum!

I help Mommy set the table.
I fold pretty napkins and put them on our plates. Mommy's baking an apple pie.
Daddy is making a big pot of steaming soup.
In a little while it will be time to dress up in our special Christmas outfits.

Ding-dong!

Hurrah! Our family is here!

"Hi, Grandma! Hi, Grandpa! Hi, Sally!"

Everyone has brought shiny Christmas presents.

They put them under the tree with the presents

we have for them.

Whoopee, let the party begin!

First we all get something to drink and we make a toast—Merry Christmas and lots of luck in the new year!

We sit down at the table.

Sally likes the way her napkin is folded.

"I folded it like that just for you, Sally."

After Daddy's soup, we eat turkey

and vegetables and potato croquettes.

It's all extra-delicious!

After pie and ice cream for dessert, it's finally time to open the Christmas presents! Sally is really happy with my present. "This necklace is so pretty!" she says, and she puts it on. "Thank you, Cousin Kevin."

Christmas is a happy holiday:
Delicious food, a tree filled with sparkling lights, lovely presents ...
But the most fun of all is laughing, talking, and sharing the holiday with my family.

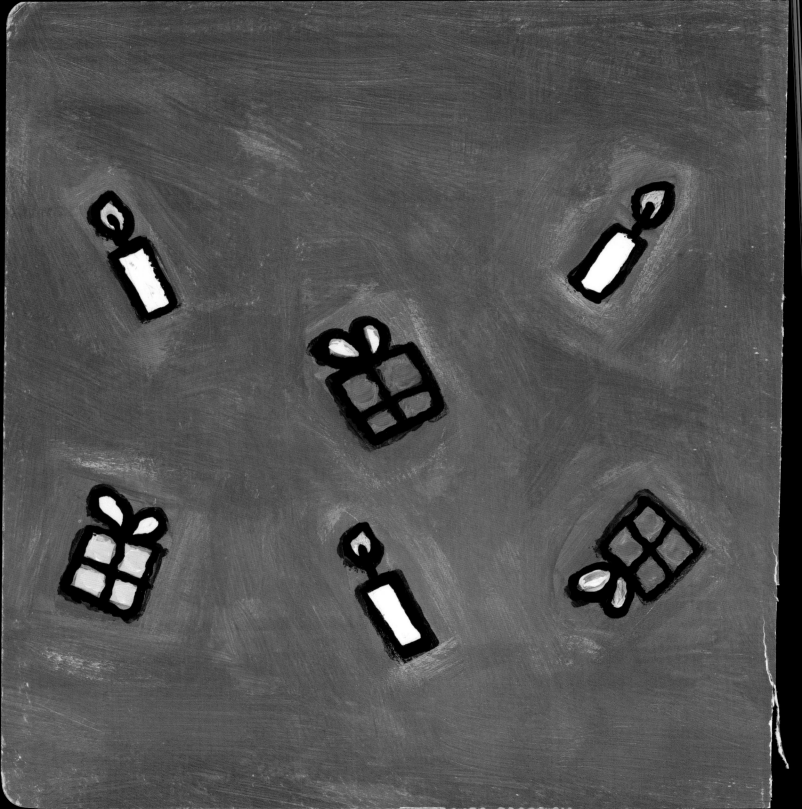

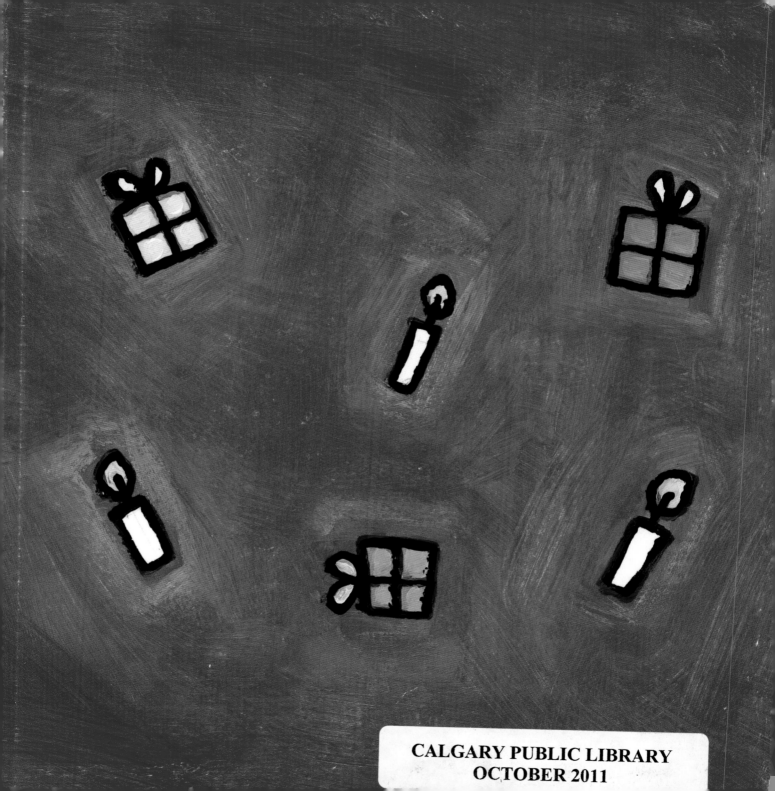

Other books about Kevin and Katie

Katie Discovers Summer
Katie Discovers Winter
Katie Goes to the Doctor
Katie Helps Mom
Katie Moves
Kevin and Katie
Kevin Discovers Autumn
Kevin Discovers Spring
Kevin Goes to the Library
Kevin Goes to School
Kevin Helps Dad

First published in Belgium and Holland by Clavis Uitgeverij, Hasselt – Amsterdam, 2010
Copyright © 2010, Clavis Uitgeverij

English translation from the Dutch by Clavis Publishing Inc. New York
Copyright © 2011 for the English language edition: Clavis Publishing Inc. New York

Visit us on the web at www.clavisbooks.com – www.liesbetslegers.be

Kevin's Christmas written and illustrated by Liesbet Slegers
Original title: *Karel viert Kerstmis*
Translated from the Dutch by Clavis Publishing
English language edition edited by Emma D. Dryden, drydenbks llc

ISBN 978-1-60537-104-7
This book was printed in May 2011 at Hung Hing Printing (China) Co.,
Ltd in Hung Hing Industrial Park, Fu Yong Town, Shenzhen, 518103 China

First Edition
10 9 8 7 6 5 4 3 2 1